# GRACIAS

## The Thanksgiving Turkey

by Joy Cowley

illustrated by Joe Cepeda

SCHOLASTIC INC.

New York Toronto London Auckland Sydney

*For my editor, Phoebe Yeh,*
*who brings out the best in a story.*

*—J.C.*

*For Juana.*
*Thanks for finally finding me.*

*—Joe*

ISBN 0-590-46977-0

12 11 10 9 8 7 6 5 4                                     2/0

Printed in the U.S.A.                                    14

First Scholastic paperback printing, October 1998

The display type was set in Papyrus.
The text type was set in Benguiat.
The illustrations are oil paintings.

"MY DAD SENT ME A PRESENT!" Miguel told everyone at school. "I'm going with my grandmother to the train station to pick it up."

"That's exciting, Miguel," said his teacher. "Do you know what it is?"

"Maybe Rollerblades. Maybe a baseball glove," said Miguel. "It's from my dad, so it'll be something really good."

Miguel's best friend Clarene said, "You know about Miguel's dad? He has a big red–and–silver truck with eighteen wheels, and he drives across the country in it."

Abuela and Tía Rosa went to the train station with
Miguel.

There was a large box with holes in it. Through one
of the holes poked a head with a beak and eyes.

"It's a bird!" cried Miguel.

On top of the box was a message: *Fatten this turkey for Thanksgiving. I'll be home to share it with you. Love from Papá.*

When Miguel's grandfather saw the turkey, he said, "Where can we put a turkey? A New York City apartment is not a farm."

"*¡Qué problema!*" said Tía Rosa. "That brother of mine is *loco!*"

Miguel said, "I love my turkey. I'm going to call her Gracias."

In the end, Abuelo said Miguel could keep the turkey.
"But she must have a house. *¡Venga!* We will make her a
cage in the backyard where she can talk to the pigeons."

At the library, Miguel found a book about turkeys. He read that turkeys were grazers. They liked grain, but they also ate green plants.

Clarene and Miguel went to Central Park. They talked to the park ranger, and he gave them sacks of cut grass.

Mr. and Mrs. Chatterjee saved old lettuces and cabbages from their store. Soon the whole neighborhood knew about Gracias.

"Hi, Clarene! Hi, Miguel!" said Police Officer Deveraux. "Is that turkey getting fat?"

"Yes, ma'am," said Miguel.

"When she gets too big for your oven, give her to me," said Officer Deveraux. "I've got a bigger oven."

As Gracias grew, she became Miguel's *amiga*. She made a gobble gobble noise every time she saw Miguel, and she ate from his hand. Abuela told Miguel, "You can take Gracias out of her cage as long as you clean up after her."

Miguel wanted to take his turkey out for a walk in the street. Abuelo made a ring to fit on the bird's leg, and he tied a cord to that ring.

"Now she will not fly into someone's oven," Abuelo said.

Miguel worried when there was talk about ovens. He wrote to Papá. *Can we get another turkey for Thanksgiving? One that is dead already?* But there was no reply.

At church Miguel lit two candles, one for his father and one for Gracias. "Please, Señor," he prayed, "keep them safe."

Tía Rosa also lit a candle. *"Pobre niño,"* she said.

The leaves fell from the trees. The weather grew cold.
Abuela made a cover for the cage.

"Why bother?" said Abuelo. "It is nearly Thanksgiving."

"People shouldn't eat pets," said Miguel.

"She's a turkey," said Abuela. "That's what turkeys
are for."

"We're *amigos*!" cried Miguel. "I love her!"

"I told you it would be a problem," said Tía Rosa.

On Saturday afternoon, Clarene came over to watch
football with Miguel. Suddenly there was a noise, louder
than the television.

Miguel jumped up. "Gracias!"

The kids ran outside. The cage was empty. A boy was running down the street, the big turkey flapping under his arm.

"Gracias!" yelled Miguel.

"You bring that turkey back!" shouted Clarene.

Everyone helped Miguel and Clarene look for Gracias, but no one could find as much as a feather.

Mrs. Chatterjee said, "How could someone steal your turkey? That's terrible!"

"No worries!" said Mr. Chatterjee. "I have frozen turkeys in the shop. I give you one for free."

Miguel shook his head and began to cry.

"Let's go home," said Clarene, holding his hand.

That night, there was a knock on the door. Officer Deveraux held a bag that shook and went gobble gobble.

"Gracias!" yelled Miguel.

"I found this turkey in a no parking zone," said Officer Deveraux. "I had to arrest her."

Miguel took Gracias and hugged her.

Officer Deveraux said, "If I were you, I wouldn't leave a fat turkey in your yard. This time she got away. Next time, she's gravy."

"Yes, ma'am," said Miguel.

Abuela said Gracias could stay in the bathroom. "You have to clean out her cage every day."

Abuelo said, "I have to shower with a turkey? *¡Ay, ay, ay!*"

Miguel moved the cage to the bathroom and put a holy medal in it. "So nothing bad happens to you, *mi amiga*," he said.

The next morning, Miguel was playing outside with
Gracias when it was time to go to Mass.
"Get your jacket!" said Abuela. "I will put the bird away.
Hurry! Hurry! We'll be late for *la misa*!"
But in the rush, Abuela forgot about Gracias.

Padre Jaime was saying prayers when there was a gobble gobble gobble in the aisle. Gracias was looking for Miguel.

Everyone laughed. Miguel was very embarrassed. He left
the pew and picked up Gracias.

Padre Jaime said, "Is this your turkey, Miguel?"

"Sí, Padre," said Miguel. "Lo siento, Padre. She must have followed me."

Padre Jaime smiled. "God made small boys and God made turkeys. Stand still while I give you both a blessing."

When they got home, Abuelo laughed and ruffled
Miguel's hair. "Chicken for Thanksgiving dinner!" he said.

"Chicken?" said Miguel.

Abuela said, "No one can kill a turkey that's been blessed."

"You think Papá will like to eat chicken?" Miguel asked.

"If he is here," said Tía Rosa.

Abuela looked at Tía Rosa. "*Sí, sí*, he will like the chicken,"
she said.

The Thanksgiving Day parade had brass bands and balloons as big as houses. Miguel sat on Abuelo's shoulders so that he could see everything, and some clowns on stilts threw confetti over him.

"Did Papá like parades when he was as big as me?" he
asked Abuelo.

"Sure! Rosita, too. I had one of them on each shoulder,"
Abuelo told Miguel.

The apartment was filled with the fragrant smells of chicken and corn bread. Abuela brought out the *salsa*.

"Please, can we wait some more?" Miguel asked.

"We have waited two hours already, *hijo*," she said.

The family sat down and watched Abuelo carve the chicken and bless the food.

Abuela lifted her glass. "I am glad for this food. I am glad for this family. I am glad for this neighborhood and for this country."

"Bravo, Mamá!" cried Tía Rosa.

Miguel lifted his glass of milk. "I am glad for Papá, and I am glad for Gracias."

Abuelo said, "Where is that bird?" He left the room and returned with Gracias.

Abuelo put Gracias on the chair next to Miguel and set a plate of corn bread in front of her. Gracias ate from the dish. Peck, peck, peck. "Now we have turkey for dinner," Abuelo laughed.

"We talked to some people at a petting zoo," Abuela said to Miguel. "They will make a home for Gracias."

"A zoo?" said Miguel.

"You can visit her every week," said Abuela.

"And I will not have to brush my teeth with feathers," Abuelo said.

After dinner Miguel sat on the floor and put Gracias in his lap.

"Zoo turkeys don't get eaten," he told Gracias.

He yawned. His stomach was full of chicken and corn bread, and he felt sleepy. "I'd get to see you every Saturday," he said.

Miguel yawned again. His eyes were closing. Too-oo-oot!
Too-oo-oot! Gracias flew up squawking in fright. Too-oo-oot!
Miguel ran to the window.

Parked outside was his father's big red–and–silver truck.
Papá was home.

## GLOSSARY

| | |
|---|---|
| *Abuela* | grandmother |
| *Abuelo* | grandfather |
| *amiga* | (female) friend |
| *amigos* | friends |
| *Gracias* | thank you |
| *hijo* | son |
| *la misa* | Mass |
| *loco* | crazy |
| *lo siento* | I'm sorry |
| *Mamá* | mother |
| *Padre* | Father (priest) |
| *Papá* | father |
| *pobre niño* | poor boy |
| *salsa* | sauce |
| *sí* | yes |
| *¡qué problema!* | What a problem! |
| *tía* | aunt |